# CALLING FOR SAM

## Bernard Ashley

## Illustrated by Judith Lawton

ORCHARD BOOKS

ORCHARD BOOKS
96 Leonard Street, London EC2A 4RH
Orchard Books Australia
14 Mars Road, Lane Cove, NSW 2066
ISBN 1 85213 863 7
First published in Great Britain 1987
First paperback publication 1995
Text copyright © Bernard Ashley 1987
Illustrations copyright © Judith Lawton 1995
A CIP catalogue record for this book is available from the British Library.
Printed in Great Britain by
The Guernsey Press Co. Ltd., Guernsey, Channel Islands

# CALLING
# FOR SAM

Other Clipper Street stories are:

TALLER THAN BEFORE

ALL I EVER ASK...

SALLY CINDERELLA

# Contents

## Chapter One

Nothing makes a cat run quicker on moving day than the sight of that special basket with the long steel rod. Billy's mother had said they'd leave the cat till last in case he messed in the mini-cab. They'd get him in when everything else was packed and off. But when the flat they were leaving was just empty rooms and patches up the walls, and they started looking for him, there wasn't a whisker of him anywhere. The creature which had tripped everyone over at every turn while the packing went on had suddenly done the bunk of his life.

He was Billy's cat. Sandra said she didn't care if she never saw the flea-bitten thing again for as long as she lived. And Billy knew his mother was only pretending with her lovey voice. Because the false way she called the cat wouldn't have fooled a deaf worm.

"Sam, Sam, Sam, Sam, Sam. Sa-am! Where's my boy?" Well, Billy knew. He was nowhere near. He'd got more sense. Sam no more wanted any part of Clipper Street than he did.

He didn't bother looking very hard. It wasn't as if Sam was *lost*. Billy went back into his bedroom and sat down in the corner, by his toy cupboard. He gave its door a sort of cuddle, just to show it how he felt. All right, it was only the bottom half of the clothes cupboard, but it was built into *his* bedroom and he'd actually painted his part of it.

*He'd* bought the football transfers for the outside, and what was inside went back all the
years of his life. It deserved him getting his
arms round it and giving it a squeeze.

The trouble was, a lot of what was in it was baby stuff. And he couldn't come out and admit he wanted to take all that with him. So it had had to go: into a black rubbish sack and out to the chute. But it had hurt, inside.

And all for what? he asked himself. A stupid house instead of a flat. A house with a garden, she kept saying, where the cat would be legal and there was a front door on the street. Well, he'd had a front door on the lift all these years and that had been good enough for him. And the council didn't give a toss about people keeping pets. Someone on the next landing had a snake. It wasn't fair!

He was very near to tears. Why didn't mothers talk to their kids about what they were doing? Just moving him like this was no different to being some parcel.

"You still trying to find that cat, Billy? You've gone quiet all of a sudden."

Quiet! He'd go quiet all right! He wouldn't ever speak to her again!

"Clipper Street!" he shouted back. "*Clipper Street!* What sort of a stupid name is that for somewhere to live?"

"Better than Dockyard Buildings, I tell you!"

Better? Billy swore—and in a sudden fit of emotion he kissed his cupboard door. Better? That's what *she* thinks, he told the transfer. What does she know about it? *This* is where I want to live.

## Chapter Two

It was good luck which caught the cat in the end. They were all ready to go—and would have gone—but the rented van wouldn't start and Uncle Steve had to get into the engine. So Uncle Brian and Billy's mother went down the road to say goodbye to the pub—and when they came back Sam was in the old kitchen having a sniff.

Then it was scratched hands for everyone, and a ball of fur for flushing down the lavatory: and Billy being given the creaking basket to carry, with the loud, angry turning going on inside it.

Clipper Street was a disappointment, even against Billy's low hopes. For a start it was nowhere near the real clipper in its dry dock by the river, and it definitely didn't look the sort of place where you could kick a ball about.

It was two rows of small houses where the front gardens had plants and flowers in them, the different doors looked as if they wouldn't stand a good shot between them, and a couple

of the houses had new bay windows stuck on the front, filled with hundreds of small panes of glass.

As the mini-cab slowed down, Billy tried to pick which house he'd take for choice: well, not for choice, the least worst. But they went on past the only one he fancied—the one with curtains like the Spurs kit—so he gave up and slipped a finger in the basket for Sam to know he was still there.

There was no mistaking the one when they got to it. It had no curtains up and there was a shining new dustbin by the front gate which said "council" as if it was written on it. Two missing tiles in the front porch had had cement just slipped over them. A piece of left-over rug was the welcome mat and plastery footprints walked down the passage.

Billy sniffed, looked round. The wallpaper went right over the bumps and smelt like school papier-mâché. New paint was everywhere, including on the glass round the windows. The light flexes were so new they didn't even dangle straight. He pulled a face. All right, the council had tried, but the bare rooms looked no more like home than new garages. He definitely didn't feel any happier now he was here.

"What's all this about a garden?" he said. He put Sam's basket down in the front room

and ran through the house to a back door with a stiff bolt. He looked out at what all the fuss had been about.

To someone used to playing in the open spaces between the flats the garden was nothing but stupid and small. A narrow concrete path led past the kitchen window, out to a square of grass which would have been small for a living room.

But there would just about have been room to practise some ball skills on it, if it hadn't been for a pile of rough stones and old flowers coming out from one corner—like a crowd rampaging onto a pitch and taking up the playing space. What grass was there would never have been much, but that heap of stones spoilt the whole thing.

Billy mooched back into the house. He'd bet the telly wasn't fixed up yet. From upstairs Sandra was moaning about her bedroom.

"A *fireplace*? Who's that for, Father Christmas?"

In the front doorway his uncles were stuck with the fridge-freezer.

"Stevie, when I say 'right' it's my right, your left, right?"

At the cupboard under the stairs his mother was fuming about the electricity not being on.

"They're *starting off* as if I haven't paid the bill!"

They were all so busy complaining they weren't giving him a job to do, so he made the best of it and took a sneaky run upstairs to have a look at his new bedroom.

It wasn't all that marvellous. He knew the one: not the big front one and not the one where Sandra was moaning. It wasn't much bigger than the one he'd had in the flat—and there weren't any alcoves, and definitely no toy cupboard. On the walls was the same nothing wallpaper as downstairs, chucking up the same school smell, and the paint was a deadly cream.

It could have been his room or an old lady's, the way it looked: they'd done up the place for no one, he thought: a space, that's all it was, and he was supposed to be all excited about it. It wasn't even a place to stay out of the way in.

## Chapter Three

He ought to go down and help, he knew that. Soon someone would either miss him or see him and get cross. There were tons of little things he could carry in. He leant against the wall behind the door. But why should he? This wasn't his move, it was hers.

Still... He didn't fancy his uncles getting on at him, especially the one he didn't know: so with bad grace he went downstairs, dropped down them in sullen twos, and tried to force a useful look on his face.

"Watch out!"

His uncles were still having a bad time

with the fridge-freezer, trying to get it past the banister post and along the passage. They eyed him up as if he were just something sticking out.

"You mind yourself, son!"

Blow 'em, then! Billy's face changed back. He went into the front room and from Sam's open basket he took his plastic football. Stupid place to put it, it could have got punctured. But he was going to give that patch of grass out there a taste of some of his skills, big enough or not. Even moving homes couldn't take those away!

He had to wait while the fridge-freezer went through the kitchen door and down a couple of steps: but with all that to-ing it and fro-ing it and swearing going on, it was no sweat getting out behind them and through to the garden.

The square of grass looked even smaller

when he had a football in his hand. There
would just have been room for a forty-forty
pitch from his old school playground, if it
hadn't been for that heap of big stones coming out into it.

But top players could practise on a pound
coin, Billy told himself—if they had to.
Getting over problems like this was one of the
things which made the good ones great.

He went onto the grass and dropped the
ball on his right foot. It felt good. He juggled

it twice—onto his left and back again—and tried to get it up onto his knee. Not quite: the ball rolled over against the fence. But that hadn't been bad, he thought. He looked round. The fence was high on all three sides so all you could see were upstairs windows: but you never knew, there could be some kid up there watching and admiring him.

He picked up his ball and went for it again: down onto his right foot for two bounces before a pass onto his left and up onto his knee: one bounce there—and then he lost it again.

But quick as you like he spotted a space on the fence and as the ball rebounded he took one step forward and caught it with a fierce half-volley. Wallop! What a scorcher! It banged like a firework on the planks of the fence—would have had a goalie in all sorts, trying to keep his hands round it.

Back came the ball and Billy started his juggling again; right foot, left foot, knee; left knee, right knee, one header—and a chance at one more in the air: but the ball had gone too far forward this time and as Billy tried desperately to get another touch it looped out of reach and hit the top of the pile of rocks. Blast! He'd have had a double hat trick if it hadn't been for those stupid stones.

Cheesed off already Billy climbed up them to get at his ball. Moodily he leant over to lift it one-handed—and it came, all too easily. A baby could have grabbed it with one hand; because it was punctured. Soft. No more than a useless handful of old plastic. Now Billy swore, at the ball and at the rock that had pricked it—some stupid sharp stone!

In a temper at everything Billy grabbed up the rock from its bed of earth and slung it round hard at the fence. Crack! Serve it right. *I'll give you bang my ball!* he thought after it. And I'm having all this up! *Footballers need room!*

"Oi!"

Billy turned round. Was that one of his uncles wanting to stick his nose in?

## Chapter Four

It wasn't. It was a man looking over from next door. And he didn't look pleased, either.

"What?"

"You trying to knock down my fence?"

Billy stared at him. He couldn't tell how old he was, with the beard: a bit older than his uncles, he thought, but not an old man. He looked quite fit and handy, which was the point.

"Your fence is the other side, son. This side's mine, an' I don't want it broke, all right?"

Billy kept his mouth shut.

"Not the place for kicking balls about, anyhow. And what you tryin' to do with that rockery?"

Now Billy saw red. Who was this bloke? He was entitled to have a go if that was his fence, but what anyone did this side of it with that pile of old stones was none of his business.

"Pullin' it down. Why?"

Now it was the man who just stared.

"Come here," he said in the end. He leaned an arm over his fence. "Come here," he told him. The arm was hairy and had a tattoo on it. Billy went. When he got nearer the man went on in a much quieter voice.

"You know who built that rockery? The old couple who lived in your house, and it took 'em years to get it like that." He had lost his hard edge, had an explaining tone to him. "The old man died years ago, but old Mrs

Varley put her life into that. Did for her back, all that bending, but she loved it. Only a pity she couldn't take it with her when she went." By looking up to the sky he told Billy that she'd died. "Those ice plants you just pulled up have been there eight years to *my* knowledge. So you keep your football for the park, son, and don't destroy someone else's work without a bit o' thought, right? At least *know* what you're doing."

His arm came further over and Billy took a step back: but it was only to point at the rock lying by the fence. "Now you put that back till you've talked to your mum about what you're destroying."

Billy wanted to say no. Like anything, he wanted to defy this nosey bloke who didn't like football. He hated him already, what a rotten neighbour to get! But he put back the rock while the man stood watching, and he dug the plants back in as well: and when he did get a defiant kick at the soft ball—out of the way up by his back door—the man had gone.

Billy was left to swear in his head at the cheek of the idiot who wouldn't know ball skills if they tripped him over. And he made up his mind that the first thing he'd definitely twist his mother into doing was getting shot of that old Mrs Varley's stonery.

## Chapter Five

How the rod could have come out of the cat basket nobody knew. Everyone had seen the basket open—one of them had even put the ball in it—but everyone had thought someone else was being sensible with Sam.

"Like what?" Mrs Drew wanted to know. "Everyone knew all the doors had to be open, for moving in. Who let him out? How could he know he lives here yet?"

"How could anyone?" Sandra moaned.

"He's done a runner," Uncle Steve reckoned. "Don't like the idea of Clipper Street."

"Gone down the chip shop's my bet."

Uncle Brian looked as if he was more hungry than worried about the cat.

But in all the don't care of his uncles and the pretending-to-be-worried of his mother, Billy was taking it very badly. Sam was his cat and he should have been responsible for him. He'd seen the basket open and he'd done nothing—*thought* nothing—about it.

If he hadn't been so full of his own troubles he'd have seen how miserable his cat must have been. Shut up in that basket to be taken to a strange place, not given any milk or water when they got there: just left. When one of the uncles had let him out by accident, was it any wonder he'd run away from the rotten house?

Already Billy had looked everywhere around. He'd been in every room and back in the van. He'd "Sam-Sam-Sam'd" in the garden and up and down the street till the name

had sounded like nonsense. And there hadn't been a sign of the sleek black cat, not a mistaken miaouw nor the shadow of a tail round a corner.

Billy had always reckoned he was tough: at least, he had till this last weekend when he'd found himself actually cuddling his toy cupboard door. Now he'd had a big disappointment over the garden, had a run-in with a rotten neighbour—and finally he'd lost his cat.

He couldn't help it, but he started to cry, and what was more he didn't care who saw it. You had to care enough about people to worry about them seeing you crying. But there wasn't a bed up yet for him to cry into and there wasn't a chair clear of clutter for curling up in, so his tears didn't last long. You need soft corners for feeling sad. Quickly he dried his eyes and decided to do something about his cat. But what?

It was Uncle Steve who put his finger on it.

"Yeah, he's definitely done a runner," he said. "He's gone back home, to his old place. That's what cats do. They go back hundreds of miles, some of 'em, walk till their legs wear short."

"Yeah?" Billy looked up. "Who said?"

"It's a known fact. That's why you keep 'em indoors till they're used to the smell of the place."

Sandra wrinkled her nose and said, "Poo!" But already Billy was at the door.

"Mum, I know my way. It's not all that far, not much more'n going swimming. I'm going back to look for him."

"I'll give you a run over in the van when it's empty," Uncle Brian offered.

"No, I'm going now. While it's light. I'll get a 177. He could just about be there by now an' he'll be looking for me...."

Nobody argued. His mother got on with the bed linen, Sandra unrolled her posters, Uncle Steve threw him some bus fare, and he went.

## Chapter Six

He started off the journey feeling sad for his
cat. It must be rotten, he thought, not to
understand what people are up to. But the bus
hadn't gone halfway when his feeling sorry
for himself began to overtake his sadness for
Sam. On his own now for the first time, really on his own and not just in another room,
his bad feelings about the move started to
sweep over him again.

As soon as the bus had passed the baths he
could have been just going home in the old
days: home to his old place, like after a swim.
The journey was the same, and no one on the

bus was to know he was going back to a place where he didn't belong. It was a wrenching, weird feeling—no one knowing he was such a different person really.

And at the bus stop by the flats it started getting worse. He saw some people he knew and who he'd probably never ever see again. He passed a tree with branches which he

knew well enough to trust his life on. He looked at an aerosol squirt he'd put on a wall himself. But now he was only a visitor. He started calling Sam to remind himself why he'd come, to stop himself feeling so bad: but it didn't help a lot. While the name was coming out, underneath everything his brain went on thinking how all the people he saw didn't

know he didn't live there any more. He'd probably get chased for something he did last week. It was like going away on holiday and coming back to people who didn't know you'd been away.

If all that had been bad, though, the worst was still to come: in the block itself, going up to his landing and passing the levels where the kids lived who'd used to be his friends. Now they were just kids who went to a different school: old team-mates who'd soon be his enemies in school football matches.

He felt sick inside. Going away that morning in the mini-cab hadn't been a bit as bad as coming back.

There was still no sign of Sam on the way up the staircases: but then the cat had always known his own landing. He could take a ride in the lift sometimes and still know which floor to come out.

And that was where Billy had the biggest wrench of all—on his own landing, the place he'd hardly left. He couldn't believe what was there, when he came to it, when he rounded the concrete corner and looked along to where the sounds of the new people could be heard.

The first thing he saw was his broken toy cupboard, out there with pulled-up bits of old lino: the doors, the painted shelves from inside, the whole thing. He could see his transfers on the front and the lines which had shown where different things went: but all chopped up and chucked out.

Now he felt numb. He stood there with his hands by his sides, a strange empty feeling in his legs and a freeze on his face. It was like being attacked; the way you never felt anything till after a fight. The axe wounds and the splintering down through the wood of

his special cupboard could have been down through him: and for a while he couldn't trust himself to take even one step forward.

At last he managed it—when a man came out of the door and threw a plastery piece of fixing-baton onto the pile.

"Yeah?" he said. "You want something?"

"No! Yes. My cat. Have you seen a cat?"

"A *cat*?" The man made it sound like the least likely creature anyone would ever see. "No, ain't seen a cat. What would a cat be doin' up here?" He compressed the cupboard remains cruelly with his boot.

"It's my cat. I lived here. I've lost him. A black one, called Sam."

"Oh." The man looked Billy up and down as if he were matching him somehow with the inside of the flat: while Billy did the same— took in the hard eyes and the bull-neck of the vandal who was wrecking the place in the first five minutes.  But he couldn't keep his eyes off his broken cupboard.

"That yours, was it?"

"Yeah. *Was.*"

"Fitted, weren't it?  One o' them things you can't move.  What is it they say—'you can't take it with you'?"

It was all Billy could do to shake his head, just a bit.

"There you go, though, that's life. All change, eh?" He looked as if he wanted to get on, to do a bit more ripping out. "I've got your address for sending on bills. If I see your cat I'll give you a bell...."

"Ta." Billy took a last look at his cupboard door. It was split in three pieces, right down through the transfers. There was nothing to salvage from the wreck and take with him, not even as a mascot. The man had gone back inside and there was a loud wrench like the heart of something being torn loose.

Billy ran along the landing and off down the stairs. Life had come back into his limbs and his feet knew those stairs like a mountain goat knows its crags. But a tight lump in Billy's throat said it would take a long time before he ever got away from what he'd seen:

and the calling of Sam's name came out a different sound around the estate.

## Chapter Seven

There was something about the motion of the 177 back to Clipper Street, though, which began to get Billy's thoughts going on wheels. An old woman pulled herself on at the market and dumped herself down next to him.

"Give you ten pence for them legs, boy. Do a swap. An' my poor ol' back... Reckon my spud pickin' days are over... " She laughed and Billy looked at her, a real goer of an old girl, but all creaked up. Who was it she sounded like? And then he realised. She could have been the old lady in his house, if that other one had still been alive: her and her stuff in her garden.

Just like him! With his cupboard! And now he saw it, suddenly. It was the same for that Mrs Varley as it was for him, because neither of them could take their things where they went. And as the bus ride went on Billy's mind dwelt on what he'd just seen on his landing. The choke of it! Didn't you get gutted when you saw someone else hacking your special thing to pieces!

Now he knew. That's what the bloke next door must have been on about in the garden: feeling bad the way the old girl would have done at seeing the rock being pulled up and chucked about. By him. He could see that now.

Pity he couldn't see his cat, too, he thought: know he was safe. As he got off the bus and ran through the side streets he hoped against hope that Sam would have turned up back at the house. Bussing all the way to the flats, looking round and coming back must have taken well over an hour—plenty of time for old Sam to roll up.

But as soon as he saw the others he knew by their faces that there'd been no sign. They were looking at *him*, to see what he had in his arms.

"Not there, young man?"

"Not there, young man?"

"He's gone the long way round, Bill, called on a few lady-friends on the way."

"He'll turn up, Billy," his mother said. "Cats do."

"Oh, yeah?" She never sounded convincing.

At least the place was looking a bit more like home. The table was in, and a few chairs; the electric people had been so Sandra was fiddling with her tapes and Uncle Brian was tuning in *Grandstand*. It wouldn't be long before the van was taken back to the hire firm and the front door got closed on everyone. Which meant, if the beds were up, that they were ready to start living here.

Somehow, since the bus, he didn't feel quite so bad. At least he was *alive* in the new place. He might not have been able to take his cupboard with him, but thank God it wasn't on account of being dead—like the old lady. He could always get another something special; she couldn't. He drew in a deep breath. If only they hadn't got that bloke for a neighbour. *And if only Sam would show...*

He went through into the garden and looked at the rockery. When he came really close he could see how cleverly all the little plants had been put into the different shapes between the stones; and he did like the way some hung down like waterfalls. It was definitely worth keeping, some of it; it just wouldn't hurt to trim it back. And perhaps they could run a hose up the top and have water coming down, like Niagara: then there'd be something to watch! They could leave room for this and still make a bit more space for practising ball skills... Billy's shoulders slumped again. Except the bloke next door would still moan every time the ball accidentally bounced on his precious fence.

Fed up again, Billy kicked a rock—but only very gently. When he looked up his mother was coming hurrying out of the house at him.

"Billy, there's a man at the door. Said he's had a word with you already today. Wants to see you. Come on. Come in, will you?" She was in her usual rush, had turned and gone before Billy's stomach had even started its twisting.

It had to be the bloke from next door. Well, he'd only kicked the stone *gently*. Billy's scare turned into temper. How could that be it—if the bloke was at the door already? So what had he done wrong now? *Looked* at the rotten stones?

## Chapter Eight

It was the neighbour. He was standing in the passage with his arms folded.

"You got a cat, have you?"

"Yeah—but..." Had Sam dug up the bloke's flowers before he ran off? Done damage? Billy's mouth tightened. Anyway, who was this person, some *lord* or something?

"Will he come to you?"

"When he wants... "

"Only there's a cat in my roof space. Black. Keeps running where I daren't tread. I heard you calling, didn't I...?"

"Sam."

"Come in and see if this is him, then, will you?"

Billy's mother and his uncles were watching all this from the front room: but the man took no notice of them. He hadn't changed his voice to make it more whiney the way some men do when uncles are around.

"You coming?"

"Too right!" Billy's face lit up for the first time since he'd heard about the move. He followed the man out through his own front door and into the other one.

He didn't know what he was expecting to see, but inside he got a surprise. It wasn't the same! The passage wasn't there, next door: there wasn't a passage and there weren't any rooms, and there weren't the normal stairs. There weren't any doors, either. All the downstairs had been knocked into one big room—and going up out of it, from the floor

up through a hole in the ceiling, was a shining black spiral staircase.

"Cor!"

But that wasn't all there was to tell someone about. There was something else surprising as well.

"Come on," the man interrupted. "Up here."

With dull, exciting clangs they twisted up the staircase, past the upstairs, to where the

spiral steps went into the loft—a place someone was making into a room.

"He's up here."

The man moved to one side and Billy
looked across the space. A light was rigged
up and dangling, so he could see where the
floorboards went only so far and then
stopped. And from over in a corner were
black fur and shadow where just one lump of
darkness, there shone two startled green eyes.
Sam's.

"He must've got in the back door when I was outside talking to you." But Billy was crawling forward on the floorboards. "Watch out. Don't step on to the plaster or you'll put a foot through." Billy didn't bother with replying. He was too busy calling his cat.

"Sam, Sam, Sam. Good boy. Good old Sam."

Behind him the man coughed on the loft dust but didn't say any more. He was leaving the coaxing to the owner.

"Sa-am. Sam. Good old Sam."

It took a long time: a lot of nearly coming out and then going back: a few *Sams* said in an exasperated voice. But when Billy started a siss-siss-sissing sound through his teeth, Sam decided to take a chance, and, one soft pad at a time, he came along the joists to the boy.

"Good boy, Sam. Good boy."

And a minute or so later the three of them were back downstairs, with Sam held tight against Billy's chest—and more than the one heart thudding: because now Billy was looking round and wanting to talk about the something else that was special about the man's room.

Football trophies. Hundreds of them, it seemed. Golden columns with kicking figures on the tops; shiny globes; cups and shields; plaques; ribbons; a hard, signed ball; and a white number nine shirt.

The man was smiling. "Ex pro, you've got here son. Two London clubs and the F.A. coaching badge!"

Billy swallowed: didn't know what to say: stared.

"Don't bother, you won't know my name. We're not all famous, you know. But if you ever want a few tips, up the park, you and

your mates, I'm your man.  All right, er...?"

"Billy," Billy told him.

"Sammy Roberts," the man said.  "Sam. So tell your mum to watch out when she calls that cat!"

Billy smiled. "Yeah," he said. "Ta." And, suddenly not quite sure which way his feet went, he carried the cat indoors.

All at once he was on a high about having his pet back, and not nearly so down about the move. Perhaps Clipper Street wouldn't be so bad.

In fact, the more he thought about it, the more he was definitely looking forward one day to him calling that other Sam in—to pick up a ball and go up the park for a game.